Ella May
DOES IT HER WAY!

For Oliver, Marlene and Frieda, with love. – A. S.

Quarto is the authority on a wide range of topics.

Quarto educates, entertains and enriches the lives of
our readers—enthusiasts and lovers of hands-on living.

www.quartoknows.com

First Published in 2019 by words & pictures,
an imprint of The Quarto Group.
The Old Brewery, 6 Blundell Street,
London N7 9BH, United Kingdom.
T (0)20 7700 6700 F (0)20 7700 8066
www.quartoknows.com

A catalogue record for this book is available from the British Library.

ISBN: 978 1 78603 904 0

9 8 7 6 5 4 3 2 1
Manufactured in Guangdong, China CC042019

MIX
Paper from
responsible sources
FSC® C008047

MICK JACKSON   ANDREA STEGMAIER

Ella May
DOES IT HER WAY!

words & pictures

Say hello to Ella May.
A girl who does things her own way...

Likes dinosaurs

Likes insects
(but not beetles)

Likes stripes
(and apples)

This is her mum

This is her home

One ordinary day, Ella's mum gave
Ella something different to eat.
It looked, and smelled, *unusual*...

"Just try it," Ella's mum said.
"It's good to try new things."

Ella quite liked this idea.

So later
in the park,

Ella tried walking backwards.
Just to see what it felt like.

It took a bit of getting used to.

Up in her bedroom, Ella tried reading a book backwards. Which changed things quite a bit.

Then, after dinner,
she went backwards
up to the bathroom.

And slept backwards.
Just to see how it felt.

The next day, Ella had lots of backwards adventures in the playground.

This seemed to cause quite a stir with the other children.

Ella's mum hoped that sooner or later
Ella would get tired of walking backwards.

But once Ella had set her mind on something...

...she liked to see it through.

So a few days later, when
Ella and her mum were
walking home from the shops...

Ella's mum turned around and
walked backwards next to Ella.
Just to see how it felt.

They passed the twins from down the road.
"That looks like fun," one said to the other.
"Can we have a go?" they asked Ella.

They passed Mrs Mercer...

...Graham's grandad...

...and Big Dave
and his dog.

They all wanted
to join in too.

Before long, a huge backwards-walking
parade was marching through town.

But when they reached the bottom of the street
Ella stepped to one side and stopped.
She watched everyone walk away backwards,
disappearing over the bridge.

"Is something wrong?" Ella's mum asked.
Ella thought for a minute.
"I think I'm done with walking backwards," she said.

They set off again for home,
walking forwards, side by side.

Ella's mum was secretly
relieved that Ella wasn't
walking backwards anymore.

That is until...

Ella started doing cartwheels instead!
"Try it, Mum!" she said.
"It's good to try new things!"